Smooc a Smoocher

by Janelle Cherrington
illustrated by Larry DiFiori

 MUPPET PRESS
A GOLDEN BOOK • NEW YORK

Golden Books Publishing Company, Inc., New York, New York 10106

Of all the things Smooch loved to do, it was kissing that made her the happiest.

She loved kissing her creechers. But the creechers weren't too crazy about being kissed— at least not by Smooch.

The reason the creechers didn't love it was because Smooch had a special smoocher on the end of her nose. This smoocher made Smooch's kisses twice as strong as regular monster kisses.

In fact, her kisses were so powerful that they often left bald spots behind. Worse still, the bald spots could take a full week to grow back! And that's why Smooch's friends found her kisses rather . . . annoying.

One day Smooch was walking to her favorite patch of tickletoe trees, just past the soggy meadow in the great foggy bog. The trees shaded the best places to nap in all of Ovadare, and Smooch was tired.

But when she bent down to lift the branches of her favorite tree, Smooch was surprised to see . . .

a brand new bunch of baby creechers!

"Oh, my, my, my!" Smooch exclaimed with delight. She was so happy that she turned to kiss the creecher closest to her.

All the creechers knew what it meant when she was this happy. They had to scatter quickly or be smooched bald. So scatter they did!

But Smooch still managed to catch and kiss
one of them—or so she thought . . .

Unfortunately for Smooch, the creecher she'd caught wasn't really a creecher at all. Instead, Smooch had kissed a Scurfy Hairy-Capped Polypore—a very hairy, very, very sticky Ovadarian mushroom which occasionally could be mistaken for a creecher.

So now Smooch's smoocher was stuck!

One by one, the creechers came out of hiding to see what had happened. It was such a strange sight, they could only stand there and stare.

Finally Smooch began to stamp her feet in frustration.

"Please!" she cried. "Someone go get Shooby! I need help!"

Shooby had often warned his friends about the hairy, sticky mushrooms. So as soon as he heard what had happened to Smooch, he understood the problem.

In fact, Shooby had recently built a machine
for just this sort of emergency.
"I have the very thing," he said.

So Shooby set off with his machine to help
unstick Smooch's stuck smoocher.

Unsticking Smooch's smoocher was very hard
work because Smooch was really, really stuck!
But Shooby pushed and pulled. He turned
his machine this way and that,
until at long last . . .

Smooch came loose with a loud **POP!**

"If I've told you once, I've told you at least a hundred times," Shooby said, "monsters with strong smoochers shouldn't smooch sticky mushrooms!"

Smooch was absolutely thrilled to be free.

"Shooby!" she cried. "You saved me! I'm so happy I could give you a smooch!"

Well, of course Shooby knew what **that** meant! So, just as Smooch reached for him, he stepped neatly out of her way.

Instead, Smooch accidentally smooched Shooby's machine—and it wasn't a very comfortable smooching surface!

"Smooch," Shooby said sternly, "this is how you get yourself in trouble. You've got to learn to think before you smooch!"

Smooch patted her still-tender smoocher. She knew Shooby was right.

Of course, that didn't mean she would stop smooching altogether.

But, from then on, Smooch always checked first to make sure she wouldn't be smooching any hairy sticky mushrooms. And that gave everyone else just a little more time to get out of her way!